Prudence
Wants a Pet

For my mom, Anne Fitzmaurice —C.D.
For Chandler and Alberta —S.M.K.

Text copyright © 2011 by Cathleen Daly
Illustrations copyright © 2011 by Stephen Michael King
A Neal Porter Book
Published by Roaring Brook Press
Roaring Brook Press is a division of Holtzbrinck Publishing Holdings Limited Partnership
175 Fifth Avenue, New York, New York 10010
www.roaringbrookpress.com
All rights reserved

Distributed in Canada by H. B. Fenn and Company Ltd.

Library of Congress Cataloging-in-Publication Data
Daly, Cathleen.
    Prudence wants a pet / Cathleen Daly ; illustrated by Stephen Michael
King. — 1st ed.
       p.   cm.
    "A Neal Porter Book."
    Summary: Prudence wants a pet so much that she adopts a
branch, a twig, a tire, and even a shoe named Formal Footwear,
but none is a suitable pet for Prudence.
    ISBN 978-1-59643-468-4
    [1. Pets—Fiction.]   I. King, Stephen Michael, ill.   II. Title.

PZ7.D16946Pr 2011
[E]—dc22
                                            2010022001

Roaring Brook Press books are available for special promotions and premiums.
For details contact: Director of Special Markets, Holtzbrinck Publishers.

First edition 2011
Printed in March 2011 in China by South China Printing Co. Ltd.,
Dongguan City, Guangdong Province

10 9 8 7 6 5 4 3 2 1

Prudence
Wants a Pet

CATHLEEN DALY

Illustrations by
STEPHEN MICHAEL KING

A NEAL PORTER BOOK
ROARING BROOK PRESS
NEW YORK

Prudence

wants

a

pet.

"No," says Dad, "pets cost too much to keep."
"No," says Mom, "pets make noise."

Prudence gets a pet. It is a branch.

Its name is Branch.
Prudence drags it to school.
She drags it home again.

"Branch is getting some exercise,"
says Prudence.

Branch doesn't eat much. Just a little air.
Prudence puts out a bowl of water for Branch.
So far Branch has not been thirsty.

Branch is an outdoor pet.
Branch lives on the front porch.

Branch tripped Dad.

Eight times.

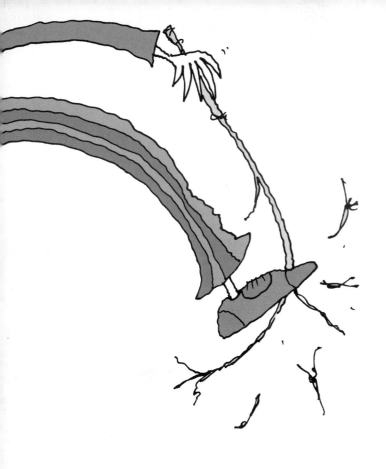

Dad broke Branch into little bits
and put them on the woodpile.

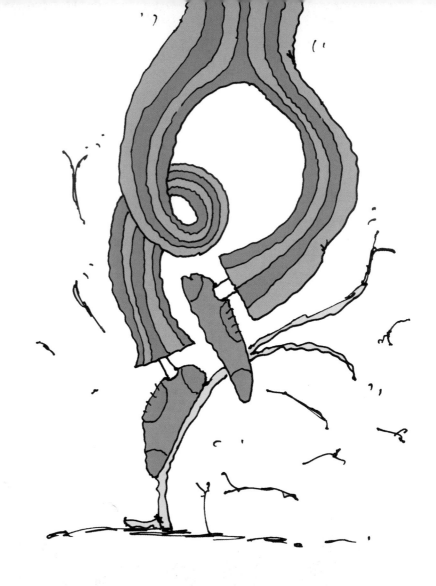

Prudence has a new pet.
Its name is Twig.
Twig lives in her pocket.

Twig doesn't need air, water,
or a porch. Twig is a miracle.

Twig ran away in the rinse cycle.

Prudence put up a notice in the laundry room.

LOST PET
TWIG is the name.
Small and brown.
Really small.
Call 555-9292

So far no one has called.

Prudence wants a pet.

"No Pru," says Dad, "there's not enough space."

"No," says Mom. "Did you clean your room yet?"

Prudence gets a new pet. It is an old shoe.
Its name is Formal Footwear. She found the name
written on its inside.

She puts Formal Footwear on a leash and
takes him for a walk around the block.

The neighbors find Formal Footwear very interesting. Prudence shows them all the tricks she has taught Formal Footwear. Formal Footwear is a smart shoe.

Soon Prudence gets tired of taking Formal
Footwear on walks and making him do tricks.

Formal Footwear never licks Prudence.
Or jumps in her lap.

Prudence frees Formal Footwear in the
junkyard. She knows Formal Footwear
will be happier there.

Prudence finds a new pet. It is her brother. His name is Milo. She puts Milo in a box with some water.

Prudence washes her new pet. She dries him and brushes his fur.

Doesn't Milo's bow look nice?

Her new pet Milo is hungry.

She feeds him some seeds and grass.

Milo doesn't feel very good. He won't stay in his box.

Mom and Dad are mad at Prudence. Grass is not for boys. Milo is a little green. Prudence is very sorry.

Prudence wants a new pet.
"No," says Dad, "we've been over this."
"No," says Mom, "pets are messy."

Prudence finds a new pet. It's a car tire.

His name is Mr. Round. It's hard to roll Mr. Round
straight. He rolls this way and that way.

Whoops. The neighbors aren't
pleased with Mr. Round.

Mr. Round is getting harder to roll. And to carry.

Mr. Round is big. Prudence is small.

Mr. Round finds a new home in the vacant lot.

He will have friends there.

Prudence needs a new pet.
She sees an ad for sea buddies.
"Yes," says Mom, "you may get those."

They come in a package and are dry
like Kool-Aid to be mixed with water.
Dry animals in a package? They
come to life in water?
Prudence is so excited she can
hardly stir.
Prudence watches the water.

One day passes,

then two.

Something is growing.

It looks like pulp.

Like fresh-squeezed orange juice.

But not orange.

"Those are the sea buddies," says Dad.

"The pulp?" says Prudence.

"Yes, I believe so."

Prudence goes to live in the closet
for the rest of the day.
She was hoping the sea buddies would
have faces. Or move.

"Prudence really wants a pet," says Mom.
"Yes, she does," says Dad.
"Hmmmmm," says Mom.
"Hmmmmm," says Dad.

"Somebody's birthday is next week," says Mom.
"Hmmmmm," says Dad.
"Hmmmmm," says Mom.

KEEP OUT

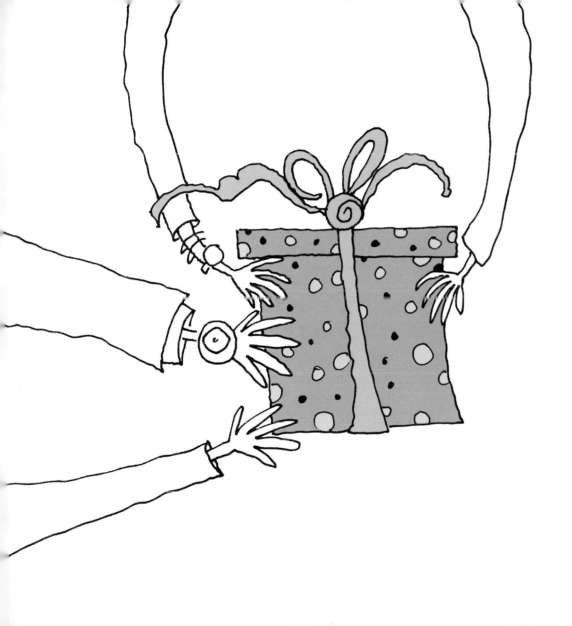

Prudence gets a big, pink birthday present.
It has holes in the sides. It makes a noise.

"Mew."

Prudence stands up and jumps up and down eight times. Her eyes get hot and tingly. She's so happy it leaks out of her eyes a little. She didn't know about those kinds of tears.

"Aren't you going to open it?" says Mom.

Prudence lifts up the lid. There it is. Her very own ball of brown fluff. She squeezes and squeezes, but not too tight. She snuffles and kisses. He is skinny and brown with little legs like twigs.

"What will you name him?" asks Dad.

"Branch," says Prudence.